GLASSES

Written and illustrated by Bob Reese

CHILDRENS PRESS®
CHICAGO

Thanks to my wife, Nancy, for her ideas and help in writing "School Days." A special thanks also to Fran Dyra for her inspiration and editing.

Library of Congress Cataloging-in-Publication Data

Reese, Bob.
    Glasses / written and illustrated by Bob Reese.
      p.   cm. — (School days)
    Summary: A young boy has trouble seeing at school until he gets glasses.
    ISBN 0-516-05580-1
    [1. Eyeglasses—Fiction. 2. Schools—Fiction.
3. Stories in rhyme.] I. Title. II. Series: Reese, Bob.
School days.
PZ8.3.R255Gl   1992
[E]—dc20
                                    92-12185
                                        CIP
                                        AC

WELCOME TO
MISS NATALIE'S
CLASS-ROOM 21

Hi, this is me in one of my classes.

4

This is how things looked
before I wore glasses.

It was hard
to see friends,

6

because they
were blurs.

It was hard
to see teachers.

It was hard
to read words.

Then I met a girl who said to me,

"Go tell your mom
that you cannot see."

I told my mom,
"I cannot see."

Mom had the doctor test my eyes for me.

The doctor said,
"You cannot see.

The doctor made
glasses just for me.

My glasses are great.
They help me see.

It is great
to see friends

18

when they
are not blurs.

It is great
to see teachers.

It is great
to read words.

HI,
MY NAME
IS MISS
NATALIE.

And the girl who helped me see

is really, really pretty.

WORD LIST

a	great	mom	they
and	had	my	things
are	hard	not	this
because	help	of	to
before	helped	one	told
blurs	hi	pretty	was
cannot	how	read	were
classes	I	really	when
doctor	in	said	who
even	is	see	words
eyes	it	teachers	wore
for	just	tell	you
friends	looked	test	your
girl	made	that	
glasses	me	the	
go	met	then	

About the Author

Bob Reese lives with his wife Nancy in the mountains of Utah with two dogs and five cats. They have two daughters, Natalie who is a resource teacher in Utah and Brittany who is studying to be a dancer in New York City.

Bob worked for Walt Disney and Hanna Barbera studios and has a BA degree in art and business.